The fragrant book

© Nathanaël AMAH , 2021(**J9CR2M2**)

Cover : The author.

The fragrant book
© *Nathanaël AMAH , 2021 NATHAM Collection*

From the same author :

(E-books &   version papier)

- Somewhere in Vladivostok
- Harcèlement   (*éd. BOD*)
- Harassment   (*éd. BOD*)
- Acoso   (*éd. BOD*)
- Neith (La mystérieuse Nubienne)   (*éd. BOD*)
- The Nubian (The mysterious Neith)   (*éd. BOD*)
- Les macarons   (*éd. BOD*)
- La veuve PLYNN   (*éd. BOD*)
- Instants ultimes   (*éd. BOD*)
- Que dire de plus ?   (*éd. BOD*)
 - Cousine !   (*éd. BOD*)
 - Tu n'es pas la femme de l'homme
             que je suis   (*éd BOD*)
- The day after in London   (*éd BOD*)
- Londres : le jour d'après   (*éd BOD*)
- Ma dernière nuit en Sibérie   (*éd BOD*)
- My last night in Siberia   (*éd BOD*)
- Faces   (*éd BOD*)
- Facettes   (éd BOD)
- GESICHTER   (éd BOD)
- Le livre parfumé   (éd BOD)
                (www.bod.fr)

« *The woman is a flower that only gives her perfume in the shade.* »

(Buddhist wisdom)

The fragrant book

THE FRAGRANT BOOK.

Novel

The fragrant book

1

"Commercial Strategy" department on the premises of a major group in the district of Paris La Défense.

On the fourteenth floor of the North Tower, the excitement of the big days: general rehearsal before the arrival of ISO experts for the renewal of ISO 9002 certification. *(production, installation, assistance, after-sales service).*

On the fringes of this event which creates a palpable tension *(the renewal of the certification being the top priority.)*, the international development is in a critical phase.

Indeed, the Chinese competition makes the management of the group sweat, and the fireman in charge of putting out the fire: Roland!

Roland P. , head of division, the group's rising star, is this frail person with red hair and a goatee of the same colour, who can be seen in all the meetings from morning to night.

He is the one who arrives before everyone else and leaves after everyone else.

This is the person to whom the Managing Director usually calls at 11 p.m., regardless of the late hour.

He is the one who is asked by the CEO to reflect on an idea that has just crossed his mind in the middle of the night.

He is the one who does not know how to say "NO".

One day came what should happen.

The Burn out.

At the beginning of the week, after a busy weekend and barely three hours of sleep *(as usual)*, Roland was unable to get up and get ready to go to work.

He is bedridden in a state of extreme fatigue.

His eyes are riveted to the ceiling of his room, his arms folded over his chest. He is having trouble breathing. His ears are ringing.

His blood pressure is vertiginous, He doesn't understand what is happening to him. He has no more juice. He is unable to react.

He seems to be "unplugged".

The caretaker of the building, who comes to clean and iron twice a week in his flat, soon realised the seriousness of the situation.

The fragrant book

SOS Doctor called to his bedside, makes the diagnosis and prescribes a complete rest to the great satisfaction of the caretaker who knows a little about the life of this tenant whom she considers as her son.

If her son had escaped the car accident that killed him, he would have been Roland's age, on which she has put all her affection.

Thanks to Roland's presence in her life, she was able to overcome the alcohol addiction that had cost her her job.

The life of this brave lady has been a succession of dramas. Her son perished in a traffic accident, her husband, who could not bear the loss of his son, allowed himself to die in the true sense of the word.

These two dramas, one after the other, got the better of her aversion to alcohol. Her dad was an alcoholic and her mum had been very unhappy for years.

So, from morning to night, she did not sober

up. Her savings, then her house, everything was swallowed up in alcohol.

Then, against all odds, she ended up as a building caretaker. Lucky for her. She had spent a few nights under bridges in Paris in an advanced state of physical decay.

2

Despite the doctor's prescription, telephone calls continued to come in, morning, noon and evening.

Roland, like a well-trained but nevertheless diminished soldier, continued despite everything to give his advice by phone, to the great despair of his guardian angel, Mom Christine.

When she brought him some soup one

evening, Mom Christine found him more and more exhausted. His complexion is pale. He can barely stand upright. On his bed, scattered files testify to this intense activity which never ceased despite his sick leave.

So she decided to take the bull by the horns. Something has to be done.

It is no longer the caretaker, but the dummy mother who has decided to act. It is no longer the tenant, but the dummy son who must obey his mother.

Her decision is made. Roland must leave Paris.

But to go where?

Probably in a remote corner of France, far enough away so that, he cannot connect to a phone network.

A corner of France with three or four houses, two or three cows in the meadows, a dozen sheep, an assortment of mosquitoes and flies not too shy, a church in the middle of the village, a butcher's shop, a grocer's shop serving as a bread deposit and *(it's essential)* greenery as far as the eye can see. Oxygen, lot of oxygen, that's all. Nothing else.

Roland needs to get off the radar.

Mom Christine thinks for a moment, and remembers one of her cousins who owns a guesthouse in the country.

Roland is confused.

He has always lived in Paris. He doesn't know much about the countryside.

Moreover, for him "countryside" = "cow dung", = "flies, mosquitoes, insects, ...", = "bad smells" etc. ... .

No better in Paris with the daily emissions of exhaust fumes, but that's okay. For him, Paris is Paris. Nothing can replace Paris.

He is typically Parisian and viscerally urban.

He was born in Paris, he studied in Paris, he

works in Paris la Défense. So for him, leaving Paris would be a real uprooting and he doesn't feel ready to leave this city even for one or two weeks.

Dominating this fear is beyond his strength. Yet, looking closely at his lifestyle *(which boils down to giving countless hours of his time to this enterprise that sucks him to the marrow, even on his sick bed)*, it is difficult to understand this reluctance to leave Paris to regain his health.

Coming from immigrant parents from Eastern Europe, Roland had heard so much from his mother about the horrors of the uprooting she suffered when she left her native Georgia.

Her stories had had such an effect on him that he made anchoring an art of living, like a mollusc that attaches itself and holds on to the first rock in its path despite the violence of the waves crashing against it.

The frustrations of his mother, who had not managed *(or wanted)* to return home, left a

The fragrant book

deep impression on him.

Specialists in psychology will be able to explain in more scholarly terms this feeling of loss when people are suddenly confronted with the need or obligation to shed their past, starting with the voluntary or forced forgetting of their mother tongue.

Roland had never heard Russian spoken at home.

A desire for his parents to protect him from being torn apart when events occur that may cause him to experience the anxieties they themselves experienced on arriving in France.

Mom Christine's unexpected proposal is beginning to worry him.

He is on the verge of being unpleasant to her, of telling her in his own way, of taking care of her business *(to remain polite in spite of everything)*.

But his good education, his propensity to always say "yes", prevented him from creating a trouble with Mom Christine who would not have understood his attitude. She would have been very disappointed, even saddened.

Then, very courageously, he looked at this woman who has decided to save his health.

While she continued to dust the sofa cushions while Roland ate his soup, she said to him :

- « *My cousin lives in a charming village that you will like.* »

- « *Wher*e *?* »   replies Roland.

- « *You'll find out soon enough my boy. I'll try to get free on Friday to take you there. ... In the meantime, shut your phone and try to get some sleep. Is that understood?* »

Roland sighs deeply.

He doesn't like that.

3

After mom Christine's departure, Roland is plunged into an indescribable and unexplained anguish.

The idea of his leaving for the countryside is not made to reassure him.

But what to do?

"No" quite simply, even to this dummy

mother who has arisen in his life and who wants to protect him like the flesh of her flesh, against all odds.

But instead, it is impossible for him to find the right arguments to oppose the common sense proposal made by mom Christine, the guardian with a big heart, the queen of invigorating soups.

By Friday, he has three complete days to find the answer. But in the meantime, he needs to regain his strength. He turns off his phone and goes to bed.

To sum up :

- dotted night.
- endless night.
- nightmare night.
- rough night.
- crisis of anxiety.
- cold sweats.

Terrible night indeed, if by definition the night is made for resting.

Roland ends his night sitting in bed, leaning against the wall, empty, haggard, his eyes tired and bloodshot.

This cannot last.

The day finally dawns. It was about time.

The temptation to turn on his phone, taps him.

So he lets himself be tempted.

Safe from "prying eyes", he turns on his phone.

A dozen messages from the Managing Director.

Should he listen to them? Should he ignore them?
What if mom Christine is right?

Overwhelmed by this questioning, Roland does not have the strength to decide.
He feels weaker and weaker.
He goes back to bed and comes out of his

sleep in the early afternoon.

After a warm shower, he visits mommy Christine.

- « *Hello.* »

- « *Ah, it's you? Hello my little one. Are you feeling better?* »

- « *Yes. I've recovered a little bit.* »

- « *Tell me, have you eaten?* »

- « *No, but it's okay .* »

- « *Sit down, I'll make you an omelet with bacon.* »

- « *No, no! Thank you. I just came to ask you where you're taking me on Friday?* »

- « *Sit down, I'll make you something to eat.* »

Roland knows that mommy Christine is a stubborn head and that it is useless to resist her.

He pulls out a chair and settles down at the kitchen table and waits patiently in a religious silence, interspersed with the noise of kitchen utensils handled by mother Christine who is busy at the stove.

A few moments later, the omelet is ready. It is thick, delicately golden. It smells good. It makes you hungry. Two slices of rye bread and a glass of red wine accompany this snack.

Mommy Christine sits in front of him, and watches him eating with great appetite.

She wipes away a tear.

She imagines her son sitting in the same seat. She imagines his smiling face at this moment of the tasting of this omelette with bacon, prepared with infinite tenderness.

At the time, rabbit with mustard was his favorite dish.

She would give her life for his own.

She would give her life so that the last time her beloved Roman shared a meal with her, could not be the last.

She is inconsolable.

Her suffering is immense. The wound has not closed. Quite the contrary.

She does everything to hide it from her protégé.

She must remain credible, at all costs.
She has to be strong in front of this young man who is weakened and whom she has decided to save.

4

Friday in the middle of the afternoon.

Mom Christine's car has just stopped in front of her cousin's guesthouse, already informed of their arrival.

On board, Roland finds it hard to realize that he is indeed a hundred kilometers from Paris. What had never happened to him before, at a time when the very principle of displacement is inscribed in the DNA of his "congeners" *(human being, animal endowed with reason)*, at a time when escaping from the place of residence to breathe and reoxygenate has become a vital need for city dwellers.

Mommy Christine stays with him inside the vehicle for a while and then invites him out.

How can it be that he, Roland P, the great master of commercial strategy, an inescapable figure within the group that employs him, can be subject to vertigo in the face of the unknown?

Alain LEBLAY wrote *(in 1956)*:

" ***The unknown only causes anguish if one becomes aware of its existence.*** "

We know that one of the virtues of knowledge is to make it possible to apprehend the unknown, and that this depends on the ability of each living being *(human or animal)* to want *(voluntarily or by necessity)* to take this step to understand and apprehend what is unknown to him and which consequently escapes his understanding.

Now, according to Roland's school and university curriculum, he seems largely "equipped" for such an intellectual approach, even if, from the education he received from his parents, everything allows us to see in him a certain propensity to adopt an attitude that aims to restrict *(or even inhibit)* his willingness to go towards this unknown that frightens him so much today.

By the voice of Lana David, it is possible to add the following:

« *Behavior is communication.*
Change the environment and behaviour will change. »

Applied to Roland, it is never too late to broaden a person's mind, *(what Mom Christine does admirably)*, provided that, as some might think, that person *(named Roland)* does not belong to that category of people called "autistic" *(or judged as such)*, A category that fears abandoning its comfort zone or moving away from it, that, on the other hand, is reluctant to be confronted with what is foreign to it, and finally, that does not dare to try to overcome its apprehension in the face of the unknown.

Once again, specialists in the field will have their hands full debating this surprising subject.

Here's mom Christine out of the vehicle.

In a final effort, Roland managed to get out of the vehicle not without difficulty, taking a lot out of himself.

It is like on another planet where greenery is omnipresent. He looks everywhere. He breathes deeply. His heart beats very strongly. This overflow of emotions hugs his heart.

First steps in unknown territory, behind mommy Christine who is now in front of the entrance of the property.

- « *Roland, do you want to come in right away or take a walk around the neighborhood first?* »

- « ***I'll take a ride tomorrow.*** »

Answer completely in line with his state of mind.

5

Mommy Christine rings a bell.

A few moments later, the opening of the gate is triggered from the inside.

On the stoop, stands a woman of a certain age, all dressed in black, who welcomes them.

- « *Hello Mathilde.* »

- « *Hello Christine.* »

The fragrant book

- « *Mathilde, this is Roland.* »

- « *Hello Roland.* »

- « *Hello Madam.* »

The hostess looks at her future resident and smiles.

Mommy Christine takes her cousin by the arm and drags her away to talk to her.
Moments later, they come back to Roland who still wonders what he's doing there.

- « *Let's go get your stuff and get you settled in the studio Mathilde has reserved for you. I will sleep at my cousin's place. You will take your meals at the guest table. Mathilde will give you instructions this evening.*
Is it ok? »

- « *Ok !* » he says in a faint voice.

Then they both come out of the property to retrieve Roland's things from the trunk of the

The fragrant book

car.

- « *You'll see Roland, you'll be fine here. It's not a prison. Just a place to regain your strength and rebuild. It's important that you regain all your abilities to continue your brilliant career. When I get home, I'll go to the post office to draw up a contract for forwarding your mail to the post office. You'll see, everything will be fine. You still have three more weeks of rest. You can stay here for the three weeks.*
I'll come back for you.
Okay, buddy? »

Roland remains silent. He needs to take the blame and figure out what's going on.

He finishes emptying the trunk.

Both return into the property.

Mathilde leads them into the studio.

With authority, mommy Christine set up his stuffs, and took time off until dinner time.

The studio door closes.

Roland inspects the premises, starting with the washrooms. Then the bedding. Everything seems to be at his convenience.

So he undresses and takes a hot shower.

He has three hours before dinner.

Then he gets into bed and tries to get some sleep.

He reviews the film of the day.

He wonders about the caretaker's motivations for taking such good care of him.

He doesn't know anything about the story of this lady who will stop at nothing to get him out of trouble.

A real mother for him.

He finds it hard to admit it.

But isn't usual to said that *"resignation*

alleviates all ailments without remedy ? "

Why then, continue to put up futile resistance to the unfolding of events in an established order?

Would this be tantamount to saying a timid "Yes" to resignation? An awakened, conscious, cautious resignation, guided by the recognition or awareness of the weaknesses that handicap us and prevent us from moving forward.

Roland decided to let his guard down.

Difficult for him to do without the manifestation of this almost maternal love emanating from mommy Christine, a maternal love that could never become a false pretence, no matter what.

6

Sunday morning.

Breakfast at the guest table.

Mommy Christine watches her protégé who seems to be happy. He devours his buttered bread toast, topped with a thick layer of homemade blackberry jam. Not very dietetic, but it doesn't matter.

In front of him, a large bowl of coffee with milk that he stirs from time to time while waiting to finish eating his toast.

She is delighted and at the same time reassured to see him regain color in such a short time.

Her diagnosis was the right one and the treatment recommended and then implemented, in perfect adequacy with her observations.

Her beloved Roland, who has spent his life so far working tirelessly, to the point of losing his health, is being reborn. He regains a taste for life. This can be seen.

According to De Mélandre :

« *Blessed is he who combines health with intelligence.* »

And according to a French proverb:

« *Sleep is half of health.* »

Mommy Christine is so convinced of this that, she has made it her credo. It is therefore easy for her to instill these simple and common sense precepts to her protégé, who seems to have lost sight of these healthy living rules, at the point of seeing his health decline.

Roland's quick response to her concern to see him in good shape for the rest of his career, fully satisfies her.

But on reflection, is she right to be so involved in his life?

Isn't her empathy lulling her into illusions?

Her inordinate faith in her action as a second mother has led her to take untimely initiatives, without once asking herself if this is what her beloved Roland really wants.

Obviously, it seems to be working.

Until then, Roland, *(unaware of the drama caused by the tragic death of his son)*, allows himself to be taken advantage of.

He is a thousand miles away from knowing

the role he really plays in this woman's life, and all the good he can do for her.

Compared to his biological mother, *(a cold and bitter woman)*, he seems to appreciate all the attention he gets from this person, a building keeper, then a surrogate mother, and *(who knows)* in a more or less near future, could become a friend, a confidante.

He can measure how far he's come before reaching this point, he, the great master of commercial strategy, walled up in his ivory tower. In his way of being, he has been forced to turn back before taking the path towards this direction which opens up real prospects for the future.

Conversely, what would become of their relationship if he knew the whole truth about her drama?

Would he be indifferent to the real causes of this togetherness between him and Mommy Christine?

Nothing is less certain.

The fragrant book

It is not certain that Roland is an opportunist.

Everything he has achieved in his life has been the fruit of intense efforts. Life hasn't given him a gift so far. He doesn't know how to ask. He doesn't know how to take. He has always looked for the right way to achieve his goals.

So, surfing on the drama of a good lady to get her attention is not a trait of his character.

7

After the departure of his guardian angel, Roland decided to explore the surroundings of his resort.

A further step to take, after leaving Paris for the first time. He wants to understand the environment in which he will live for a few more weeks, during his convalescence.

To do this, he needs to bring out that other person inside him, the Roland bis, the

The fragrant book
© *Nathanaël AMAH , 2021 NATHAM Collection*

adventurous Roland, the daring Roland whose limits he ignores.

Should he be afraid of him?

Until now, the only Roland he is aware of is the one who has been trained in school, the one who measures the pros and cons before any action, the one whose rational mind systematically dismisses risky hypotheses.

Now, having taken the step towards a new way of apprehending life, consequently, he has to abandon his old life which was summarized in the "metro-work-asleep" *(sleep reduced to the strict minimum)*, for a life more fun, more adventurous, richer in emotions.

The cocoon must metamorphose into a magnificent butterfly, no matter how brief the happiness of its existence.

With a hesitant step, he is launched towards the adventure.

He takes a path which ends in a fork.

Two possibilities: on the left, the path leads to a wooded area with public benches. On the right, nothing special at first sight.

He thinks for a second and decides to take the right lane to see where it will take him.

The change of scenery is total.

Everything is green around him. He had never seen this before.

He is breathing at his full lungs. He is drunk with it. He stops in front of the groves. He looks at every flower. He doesn't hesitate to caress the petals and bend down to smell them. He sees for the first time the wild flowers described in books.
He advances at 2 km per hour, sometimes stopping to reflect on what he sees.

As he progresses, he sees on his right, the banks of a river fed by an underground spring.

Wild ducks splash around, occasionally diving for a few seconds with their heads to the bottom of the water to pull out a few treats hidden in the water.

In the distance are two grey herons frolicking and shining their plumage.

At his feet, water insects are making circles in the water. No predators to swallow them.

A little further on, a coypu is busy around a plane of rushes.
Etc ... .   Etc ... .

He is discovering the nature.

Roland spent a long time observing the abundance of life around this waterhole. His eyes looked everywhere at once. He is full of the most diverse images and sounds.

He feels free, not at all stressed. He is in wonder, in excitement.
And who says wonder, says happiness. It's a sensation he doesn't know.

Roland has *(until this very moment)* refused this luxury, preferring the abstract and austere side of an intellectual reasoning related to his favorite field, which is commercial strategy.

He had never allowed himself to be penetrated by any sensation or semblance of feeling that could make him touch with his finger what happiness is, this stable and lasting state of satisfaction.

In his existence, everything is nothing but self-denial, the result of an absence of personal life, what is, on the scale of the human race, a real tragedy.

Now he discerns something he had never felt before.

He vibrates in the face of this luxuriant nature.

This vibration generates in him an immense joy.

At the same time, this overabundance of images and sounds, this nature that surrounds him, arouses in him the great regret of never having experienced such an enchantment in his other life.

His regret is sincere and deep.

The fragrant book

8

Roland retraces his steps at the level of the fork and then takes the left lane towards the wooded area he had seen when he arrived.

With the same caution, he progresses slowly, observing every detail he can see on his way.

The wooded area is only a few meters away when he sees an object on the bench at the entrance.

The closer he gets, like an eagle, his eyes clearly distinguish the object on the bench.

He is not dreaming.

It is indeed a book.

While advancing towards the bench, he scans the surroundings. He would like to make sure that the owner of this book is not in the area.

But he realizes that there are very few people in that place at the very moment his eyes are exploring it.

Indeed, on one of the benches, a lady of a certain age, immersed in reading her book, one hand on the back of the book to hold it, the other on the reading page. On another bench, a couple takes the advantage of the fresch. In front of them, a baby carriage in which, a baby is sleeping peacefully. At their feet, a Golden Retriever on a leash, sleeping with only one eye, patiently awaits the return home.

The fragrant book

Roland no longer hesitates: he settles on the bench.

He takes a look at the cover of the book.

"LA VIE DEVANT SOI", written by E. AJAR

This title vaguely reminds him of something.

But remembering concretely what this book evokes in his memories, is not his main concern.

For the time being, his questioning is about the person who forgot or left this book on the bench on which he has just sat.

On reflection, for him, it cannot be an oversight, because it is inconceivable to forget a book on a bench in the middle of nature.

Unless it was a hasty departure.

It doesn't make sense.

Indeed, in this hypothesis, the first reflex

would be to close and take the book before getting up and leaving.

Leaving a book on a bench would be tantamount to a desire to part with an object that has a particular nature and symbolism, because of its social role on the one hand, and on the other hand, because of the intentions of the owner in doing so.

It should be remembered that the abandonment or destruction of a book is not an insignificant act.

For the moment, Roland is content to observe the book. He does not touch it. It does not belong to him. Maybe the owner is nearby, so he is waiting for him/her return. He sits to protect the book until it is returned to its rightful owner.

A hypothetical return indeed, if however, the desire to recover this *(forgotten)* book took precedence over its abandonment.

The day is declining. No one comes to claim the book.

The elderly lady puts her book in her purse, then gets up and leaves.

Then it was the turn of the couple, the baby and the Golden Retriever.

Then, he finds himself alone in this wooded area, enough to arouse some apprehension in him.

He waits for a while, then decides to leave.

He grabs the book, then returns to the studio in a hurry.

9

Back at the studio, he puts the book on his bedside table.

His state of mind has changed. He had left to discover his environment, and returns to the studio, inhabited by the idea of having received something, delivered by he doesn't know who.

He is troubled.

One has to wonder why the discovery of a book on a park bench has such an effect on him ?

He has the impression that he has brought home something he does not understand the meaning of.

Yet it is only a common, even banal object. Nothing transcendental to move the common people.

Roland is a rational being, who does not let himself be moved so easily. For him everything has meaning. His university education has shaped him to be that person who knows how to analyze things coldly, methodically.

But after this unexpected and disconcerting discovery, his behavior becomes irrational. He does not understand. He is not used to feeling emotions that he cannot explain, including the excitement that his discovery causes him.

While waiting for dinner, he tries to relax in

bed. He is lying on his back with his neck on his two open hands and his eyes glued to the ceiling.

During dinner, he remained strangely silent, having gradually become accustomed to communicating.

Solicited by some and by others, he was content to answer out of politeness. Minimum service. All his mind is turned to the book on his bedside table.

A small delay caused by the preparation of the dessert, which is late in arriving to his opinion, dramatically prolongs the dinner. He keeps looking at his watch. He is on the verge of annoyance.

And then came the moment to leave the table.

He greets everyone and rushes into his studio. He double closes the door.

He takes off his shoes, loosens his belt, then gets into bed, putting himself on his side, and having the book in his sights.

He stayed like this for a while and then straightened up. He looks for the ideal position in this bed which is not his. Finally, he leans against the wall with his back supported by a pillow. Then, he took the book with a firm hand.

Yes, the title on the cover reminds him of something.

As in the wooded park, it does not seem important to him to remember very precisely the memories that this title brings up in his memory. He will see later.

Machinically, he opens the book on the first page.

What was his surprise!

He is stunned.

A woman's perfume exhales. The emanations of a musky perfume, trapped in this book, escape and come to tickle his nostrils.

What is written on this first page is totally indifferent to him. All his attention is focused on this perfume that never ceases to torment him.

He starts to stare at the page as if, this person who was wearing this perfume, was going to appear in flesh and bones in front of him as if by magic.

This is certainly what he would have wanted to ask her the reasons for her gesture.

His attention remains frozen on this first page of the book and cannot take it off.

His imagination gallops. He sees the perfumed fingers of this person landing on the pages of this book. He sees them turn the pages, one after the other.

Then, feverishly, page after page, he searches for that same scent, bringing the book closer to his face each time, his nostrils on high alert.

On page 20, no more smell, nor on the

following pages.

 So according to the logic that had settled in his mind, the stranger with the musky scent had stopped at page 20.

 Therefore, why, having barely begun to read this book, this person felt the need or was forced to abandon it?

 What happened?

The fragrant book

10

It seems that through listening to a voice it is sometimes possible to guess the nature of the person speaking, his state of mind, ...

What can the scent of an unknown person reveal?

In learned terms: his/her olfactory signature.

This olfactory signature alone cannot justify the wearing of such a perfume and not another, on a given day.

.

It is important to add two fundamental elements: the emotion felt at the time of buying this perfume, and the mood that this person is in when choosing to wear this perfume instead of another one, on a given day.

On the other hand, a perfume will not be able to reveal if it is about a brunette, a blonde, a redhead, even less that it is about an African, a Caucasian, an Asian, woman.

The task seems arduous *(even titanic)* for Roland who would like to picture this woman whose portrait he tries to sketch from her perfume.

What about the elderly lady sitting on one of the benches in the wooded area? Was she wearing perfume? If so, what kind of perfume? Why this perfume precisely? Are the pages of the book she was reading fragrant?

How to determine the typology of people likely to wear this type of perfume?

Is there an olfactory preference by age group?

Is it the original scent of this perfume, since, depending on the type of skin, the scent of perfumes change somewhat.

Roland does not let himself be discouraged by this approach which seems *(to the common people)* an impossible mission.

For him, there must be a way to solve this enigma.

Yes, remember, Roland is the grand master of business strategy.

Yes, in that case, Strategy can be the art of developing a coordinated plan of actions, the starting point being the scent of a perfume trapped in a book.

If he succeeds, he would be fit and worthy to

The fragrant book
© *Nathanaël AMAH , 2021 NATHAM Collection*

work alongside Scotland Yard's fine bloodhounds.

Unless ... .

11

The main reason for his presence in this resort is to try to rest after his state of exhaustion at work.

However, he is beginning to feel again a certain pressure that he inflicts on himself through what he considers to be an obligation to succeed in solving the enigma of the perfumed book.

Incorrigible Roland!

The fragrant book
© *Nathanaël AMAH , 2021 NATHAM Collection*

Monday, 8 a.m. Breakfast at the guest table. Everything goes well.

At the end, he approaches his hostess and asks to speak to her.

- « *Is something wrong?* »

- « *No, everything is fine. Don't worry. I just wanted to ask you where I can find a perfume shop around here?* »

- « *A perfume shop? A perfume shop?* », repeated the hostess while reflecting.

- « *There is no perfume shop in the area as you say.* »

- « *Oh really?!* »

- « *Yes.* »

- « *Is there really no way to find one?* »

- « *Absolutely, yes, but you have to go to the city center in the neighboring town. There,*

The fragrant book

you are sure to find one. »

- « *How do I get there? I don't have my car unfortunately.»*

- « *You can go there by bus. There is a bus every half hour and it will drop you off in the city center, not far from the train station.»*

- « *Okay. Where exactly is the stop of this bus, please? I don't know the area very well as you know. »*

The hostess went away for a short while, then came back with a tourist map of the region in her hands. She patiently explained to him the itinerary to follow.

- « *Thank you very much. I won't be having lunch today at the guest table. See you tonight.»*

- « *See you tonight. »*

Roland retires and returns to his studio.

The fragrant book

As soon as the way is clear, the hostess throws herself on her phone.

- « *Christine hello. it's your cousin.* »

- « *Hello. Why are you calling me? Did something happen to Roland?* »

- « *No, don't worry.* »

- « *So why are you calling me?* »

- « *Please don't scream! I just want to talk about something.* »

- « *You worry me. Speak up!* »

- « *Your protégé asked me for the address of a perfume shop this morning.* »

- « *A perfume shop? And why? Did you ask him why?* »

- « *You're exaggerating. How can I ask him such a question?* »

- « *So how do you expect me, from Paris, to*

know why he needs a perfume shop ? »

 - « *Is your boy married?* »

 - « *No, he is not!* » shouts Mommy Christine who is quite annoyed.

 - « *Why are you getting angry? I just wanted you to know what's going on.* »

 - « *Tell me, what's going on? What's going on?* »

 - « *He left for the city.*»

 - « *Huh? Where?* »

 - « *I told you in town. He went to look for his perfume shop. I have to tell you how?* »

Mommy Christine is red with anger.

 - « *And why did you let him go? Yet I had asked you to look after him.* »

 - « *Yes, but you didn't ask me to keep him on a leash. I wanted to do the right*

The fragrant book

thing....... »

- « **When he comes back, could you tell**
him to call me? »

- « *I hope you won't tell him I told you.* »

The fragrant book
© *Nathanaël AMAH , 2021 NATHAM Collection*

12

Roland reaches the city center of the neighboring town, thanks to the indications provided by his hostess.

Somehow, he obtained from passers-by, the address of a perfume shop not too far from where he was.

He goes there diligently, with the firm hope of beginning to solve his enigma.

In front of the perfume shop, he marks the step, then decides to enter.

A saleswoman walks towards him.

- « *Good morning Sir. Can I help you?* »

- « *Good morning Madam. Yes I think you can help me... whatever... .*»

He seems hesitant. He doesn't know how to approach the subject that preoccupies him and that has pushed him to surpass himself.

- « *Sir, I am listening to you.* »

Now they are two saleswomen in front of him. Indeed, in front of his hesitation to speak, the first saleswoman discreetly signalled to her colleague who immediately approached them.

Then, he opens his briefcase (*before the amazed eyes of the two saleswomen)* and takes out the famous perfumed book.

The fragrant book

*- « **Yes, this is a delicate thing I would like to ask you: could you please smell the perfume of this book and tell me what it is? I'm looking for that perfume. Can you please help me?** »*

The two saleswomen look at each other and burst out laughing. They think of the hidden camera. But their customer seems serious and determined.

In the memory of saleswomen, they have never heard such a request from a customer.

By definition, in a perfume shop, it is the saleswoman who makes the perfumes smell, not the other way around.

Moreover, in this environment in which scents are intermingled, how to manage to identify a perfume exhaled by the pages of a book?

They don't know what to say. They are perplexed, torn between laughter and the desire to help this gentleman, who is also a nice guy.

They are saleswomen and not the "noses" of perfume creation laboratories.

A "nose" knows how to identify all the components of a perfume. It is a profession. Roland, blinded by his determination seems to ignore it.

Worried by the crowd of her saleswomen around this customer like no other, the store manager, attracted by the vocal manifestations of her saleswomen who have turned away from the other customers present in the store, comes to the news.

One of the saleswomen whispers something in her ear for a few seconds.

The situation does not amuse him at all. She seems irritated by the presence of this "wacky" customer *(according to her)*, who comes to make a mess in her store. Is he sent by the competition? She is not far from thinking so.

She turns to Roland, her face closed, her tone icy:

- « *Hello Sir, tell me, is this a joke?*»

Roland doesn't know where to stand. In his entire life, no one has ever spoken to him so harshly, so brutally.

His face becomes scarlet red. He feels tingling all over his body.

- « *Sorry.*»

he said with a knotted throat as he put the book back in his briefcase.

He comes out almost backwards from perfume shop.

He has never felt so humiliated in his entire life.

In his work, he is a big head. He is highly respected for that. His interlocutors speak to him with deference.

The fragrant book

What he has just experienced leaves a bitter taste in his mouth and a deep trouble in his mind.

He is now in the street. He quickly moves away from the perfume shop window behind which the saleswomen who continue to mock him, watching him move away.

His legs threaten to slip away from him.

He thinks of the saleswomen who are going to revel in this story *(at his expense)*, with their loved ones, after this particular moment of frank laughter during this unusual day that they have just experienced thanks to him.

It is customary to say that obstinacy is the path to success.

However, his obstinacy has just inflicted a setback on him, the bitterness of which he is not ready to forget.

13

To make a second attempt in another perfume shop, is beyond his strength.

The best thing he can do after this memorable disappointment is to go back to the studio, get away from this world whose propensity to make people suffer he has just discovered.

Periodically, the human species is confronted with a disaster of some kind.

Why should he, *(the undisputed master of commercial strategy who claims to know how to anticipate everything)*, escape this fate?

As soon as said, as soon as done: there he is, within the four protective walls of his studio. Relative security.

He had time during the bus ride to rethink his strategy. The result of this morning's experiment is not conclusive. To say that it was a fiasco would be an understatement.

However, his obsession does not wane because he knows that it is by moving forward that one discovers the problems that arise.

In particular, he discovers a temperament that cannot be controlled. He didn't know that he could dare to undertake something without a safety net, to rush headlong into a quest whose outcome could be uncertain, to look for meaning where he knows it doesn't exist.

He is unable to impose on himself the necessary inner silence that would allow him to discover and understand the real reasons for his relentlessness in discovering the owner of the perfumed book.

Why this woman who hides behind these fragrant pages haunts him so much?

In fact, he finally admits that his haunting was born out of his fear of leaving this resort without having discovered this woman.

Discovering her why? To do what with her? To satisfy what ambition?

Why this fragrant book is for him, is a call that goes far beyond his own understanding? What does it do with his ability to reason? Why does the irrational come to trouble his mind?

He is probably falling in love with a fragrance like with a woman who entering a subway train and for whom he would give up going to work in order to follow her, without knowing where it will lead him.

Isn't that dangerous?

If he fails in his attempt to personify that smell that holds him by the tip of his nose, then, once it will evaporate, what will remain of his obsession? A void? A colossal waste of time? A distress in front of the imaginary face of this untraceable, inaccessible woman who disappears forever like a soap bubble bursting in the air?

Yet it is usual *(especially in the Paris district of La Défense)* to take an elevator in which traces of the passage of a perfumed woman remain.

Does one become however a detective in search of this fragrant woman by visiting each office on each floor of a twenty-story tower, sniffing the neck of each of the women working there?

In Roland's defense, the context is different.

Indeed, it is more "normal" to meet a perfumed woman in an elevator than to find a perfumed book on a public bench in the middle of nature.

But for the moment, it gives the impression of being an animal, a dominant male hunting after having sniffed the scent left by a female during the mating season.

14

At dinner time, Roland, still under the effect of his disappointment, but trying to look good, settles down at the guest table.

By a curious coincidence, he finds himself in front of his hostess who has deliberately chosen to sit opposite him.

She stares at him. She questions him with her gaze. She can no longer stand on her chair. She is nervous. She loses her appetite, she   so greedy.

The fragrant book
© *Nathanaël AMAH , 2021 NATHAM Collection*

No reaction from her resident.

What will she be able to say to her cousin who should call her back in the evening to get news of her protégé?

She cannot bear the indifference shown by Roland who is one light year away from her torment.

She has no control over him. He is not accountable to her.

It's true: he asked her for the address of a perfume shop.   And then what happened?

And if he had asked her for the address of a bakery, would she be inclined to look him in the eye to get his opinion on the baking of the bread he might have bought?

No !

Indeed, Roland's concern is of a different nature. He is in a hurry to get back to his studio as soon as possible.

Her mobile starts vibrating insistently for the third time since the middle of dinner.

Fairly annoyed, she takes the call and says in a dry tone :

- *"I 'll call you back! "*

before her interlocutor had time to say a word.

A few moments later:

- " *Hello, Christine it's me.* "

- " *Is he home?* "

- " *Yes. He just had dinner. He has just returned to his studio.* "

- " *So?* "

- " *So what?* "

- " *What did he tell you?* "

- " *Nothing!   What do you want him to tell*

The fragrant book

me? "

- " He didn't tell you anything about the perfume shop, and why did he go there? "

- " No! First of all, stop yelling. I really don't know why you're in such a state. Besides, who is this guy for you to watch him like milk on the stove? "

- " What do you mean by this question? "

- " I'm not implying anything. Ever since you found out he went to a perfume store, you've been hysterical. I don't understand your attitude. I ask you again: Who is this person you brought into my house? "

- " It's nobody."

- " This guy is wanted by the police? "

- " No !!!!! "

- " Is he your lover? "

- " Mathilde, please don't insult me. He

The fragrant book

could be my son. "

 - " Yes, but he is not. So why do you brood him like that? "

 - " I don't brood him. Besides, you don't understand anything. Have a nice evening. "

 Seen from the outside, one can only feel sorry for the deleterious effects of the collateral damage caused by the discovery of this book with its fragrant pages.

 Two cousins who love each other and who are on the verge of getting angry forever because of an unbelievable story, it's hard to understand.

15

The night after his bitter disappointment, Roland could not sleep a wink.

Indeed, when he returned to his studio, Roland took the book and started reading it as he had never read a book like this before, used to reading mainly technical files, full of spelling mistakes.

In the course of the pages, he discovers Momo's life with Mrs ROSA, a former prostitute, guardian of prostitutes' children, close to death.

He discovers the altruistic attachment of a Jewish mother for an Arab child who is not hers and whose no one wants him anymore since no one pays the expenses of his care with her.

He discovered the story of this beautiful lesson in life and for the first time he could feel this flood of emotions that overwhelmed him just by reading a book, a book moreover: discovered by chance on a bench somewhere. Reading this book allowed him to have a beginning of explanation on the behavior of mom Christine and to understand a little more, her growing interest in him.

But the risk of being mistaken about the origin of this attachment applied to his own case, is proven.

Mom Christine sees in Roland her missing son, and decides to usurp this substitute role in order to fill the gaping hole left by the disappearance of her son Romain. She "takes" Roland by the hand and puts him in this place

The fragrant book

of honor in the depths of her heart in order to preserve him from any danger, anticipating the resolution of everything that could hinder *(or harm)* the existence of this fragile link.

As for Mama Rosa, she decides and takes the liberty of repairing an injustice caused by Momo's abandonment by his biological mother, without trying to find out whether this abandonment is voluntary or imposed by fate. It had to be done and she did it without question, thus preventing Momo from being placed in foster care by the public assistance.

Different motivations leading to the same end, namely the gift of self.

Two moms, two maternal hearts beating in unison by interposed children, reacting with a quarter turn, putting into action the maternal instinct that protects, reassures, and helps avoid life's pitfalls.

Suddenly, the sun's rays light up the studio.

Roland takes a look at his watch: 6 o'clock.

Ten more pages to read. They can wait. He is tired. It's time to go to bed.

The fragrant book

16

In the middle of the afternoon, Roland emerges from his "night".

A strong migraine. Eyes reddened by the lack of sleep. The doughy tongue. Slight loss of balance. He feels dehydrated. He still enjoys the warmth of his bed a little but unfortunately not for long.

Worried not to have seen him either at breakfast or lunch, and not to face the wrath of her cousin Mommy Christine *(who would*

The fragrant book

like to know minute by minute what her protégé is doing), Mathilde, the "nanny" in charge of Roland, comes to the news, fear in her stomach not knowing how she will be received.

She knocks timidly at the door, once, then a second time. She listens at the door and tries to detect the slightest sign of life in the studio.

A few seconds later, just enough time to get dressed decently, Roland, *(still wearing the traces of his pillow on his face)*, opens the door, dazzled by the light of day.

Standing in front of the open door, Mathilde is seized by a strong smell of women's perfume emanating from the studio.

Instinctively, she glances through the half-open door.

No woman hiding in the studio, in the light of the little she could see.

But then, where does this woman's perfume come from that she receives right in her nose?

" *Oh, who's that guy?* " she says to herself in her head.

She stares at Roland for a brief moment, then :

- " *Hello !* "

- " *Hello !* " answers Roland politely.

- " *Are you all right?* "

- " *Yes, thank you. Why this question?* "

- " *We haven't seen you all day. Is everything going well? Everything is going well? Are you all right?* "

- " *Madam, at the risk of displeasing you, I have already answered you. Everything is fine, thank you! I went to bed at dawn and slept part of the day. There, you know everything. I will be at the guest table tonight. See you later Madam.* "

He closed the door and went back to bed.

The fragrant book

For her part, Mathilde withdrew with this sentence in mind: " ... I went to bed at dawn... " which comes to add to the mystery after the puff of smell of perfume of woman breathed in front of the studio.

What will she be able to tell her cousin?

She is trembling in advance.

She runs to get a little liqueur to give herself courage before her cousin's daily call.

The fragrant book

17

Mathilde's visit had the unpleasant effect of cutting off his desire to go back to bed.

A brief passage in the bathroom, then, in the direction of the wooded area, the book under the arm to return it to its owner if necessary.

Arrived on the spot, he takes place on the famous bench and finishes reading the book.

He took his leave of Mrs. Rosa and Momo, who, despite everything, will continue to inhabit his mind for a long time to come.

The fragrant book

Indeed, the circumstances of their unexpected encounter, *(an encounter inseparable from this fragrance emanating from a book forgotten on a bench in nature)*, pushed him towards a *(almost surrealist)* universe that was unknown to him. Successively, he experienced sensations and feelings for which his previous existence had not prepared him.

The specialists will give their opinions on his future, after having lived through what he has just experienced.

In the wooded area, people come and go in this place where it all began.

He observes all these people, sometimes noisy, sometimes more respectful of the serenity of the place.

He waits.

No one comes to claim the book.

So, day after day, he made the same journey and occupied the same bench, waiting wisely for the owner of the book to come and claim her property.

In vain.

Saturday: same time slot, same route, same place.

Ah, bench in sight.

Bench occupied.

Maybe 'her' at last!

He's pressing on. His heart is racing.

No, false alarm: it is a man of a certain age, quietly smoking his cigar.

Strong smell of tobacco in the vicinity.

He wonders what he comes here to do, to pollute the air of this enchanting place, dedicated to purity and serenity of spirit, not suffocation.

Big desire to challenge him, but what's the

point? He prefers to turn back.

He will try his luck again on Sunday.

18

Sunday: fruitless day.

Monday: Roland decides to return to town.

He waits patiently at the bus stop.

A young woman comes to stand next to him.

Instinctively, Roland gets closer to her, enough to smell her perfume.

The young woman, not at all shy, smiles at him.

- " *Good morning Madam.* "

- " *Good morning, sir.* "

- " *I'm sorry I scared you. I just wanted to smell your perfume. I'm really sorry.* "

The young woman bursts out laughing.

This laughter reminds him of something. But he succeeds in extinguishing this unpleasant sensation that tries to resurface.

- " *Don't be sorry, sir.* "

Against all odds, the young woman opens her bag and removes a bottle whose design is particularly meticulous.

- " *Give me your hand.* " ordered the young woman.

Roland obeyed and held out his left hand.

Then she delicately takes his hand, turns it over and sprays her precious perfume twice on the inside of his wrist. She asks him to shake his hand for a few seconds before smelling.

Surrealist scene.

This is where his obsession led him.

This conduct can *(in times like these)* be assimilated to an aggression that could lead him into serious trouble.

But lucky for him: the young woman is in a joyful mood and not at all shy.

Such behaviour is not like him. He is an introvert and in his whole life he has never dared to make the slightest inappropriate gesture towards a woman. He does not know how to court a woman. He is not afraid of women, but he has always been restrained in front of women. His love affairs can be counted on the fingers of one hand.

He thanks her and cannot help but compare

the fragrance of this perfume sprayed on his wrist to that of the book engraved in his olfactory memory.

Too lemony. The perfume of the young lady has nothing to do with that of the pages of the book.

- " *I like it a lot!* "

he says hypocritically. In reality, extremely disappointed. Chance doesn't always do things right. It would be too good to fall at this bus stop on the one that has been driving him crazy for a few days and because of who he has suffered the most unbearable humiliation of his life.

- " *Really?* "

- " *Oh Yes!* "

- " *OK! My boyfriend doesn't like it at all. But what do you want to do about it?* "

- " *Don't hold it against him for that. You know, tastes and colors. ... You know the old saying well. Don't you?* "

The fragrant book

19

Tuesday: resumption of the daily ritual.

Five more days to solve the enigma before returning to Paris. He remains hopeful that he will succeed.

But instead of spending his time watching for the hypothetical appearance of the lady with the musky perfume, Roland decides to combine business with pleasure. He lets go and takes advantage of the leniency of weather and the environment which is no longer systematically limited to the wooded area.

For the next five days, he no longer wants to live in this permanent questioning that obliges him to make the trial of providence that has not allowed him to find the woman he has imagined since the discovery of the book on the bench.

From now on, without losing sight of the subtle and olfactory link that binds her to him, Roland understands that he has reached the limits of his waking dream to flush out this woman who will haunt him for a period of time during the next few years of his life.

He finally achieves that necessary inner silence, which allows him to put the rational back in the middle of his reflection.

He becomes again Roland P. the strategy specialist.

To take things into account in an abstract way or, to examine each constituent element of an enigma in its immediate environment?

Why hasn't the past two weeks allowed him to improve his strategy to solve the puzzle?

How can he think he can achieve this result by going to sit on a bench and wait for a hypothetical apparition, when it was simpler and more sensible to put, for example, a small advertisement on the glass door of the bread deposit?

Everybody eats bread, isn't it with or without gluten?

But the mathematical models taught in universities or in business school curricula probably do not advocate taking into account a classified ad scribbled on a piece of paper in solving a riddle of any kind.

Nice case study for first-year students.

How many will find a way to make fire in the wilderness without their lighter unless they were a youth movement at a young age?

20

After this moment of respite during which Roland briefly regained the clarity of his mind, came the torment and anguish of his return to Paris.

It is the first time in his entire life that he leaves Paris. He is therefore preparing to experience the sensations generated by his return home.

Seen from the outside, it may seem

implausible *(even silly)* to consider going home as something disturbing.

Disturbing in what way?

Disturbing because his mental path has been reversed in the manner of a change of polarity?

Indeed, the fear of discovering the countryside a few weeks ago was followed by the fear of returning to Paris to resume the course of his life.

A fear probably generated by the experimentation *(in real life)* of his biological mother's words about the torments of uprooting.

But we can legitimately ask ourselves, how can resting for three weeks in the countryside be considered as uprooting?

The negative thoughts that animated his mind as he set out for the countryside cannot be dissociated from the idea of uprooting in the primary sense of the term according to his feelings, according to his beliefs, according to his veneration of his mother.

Roland was out of his comfort zone during this trip. Very quickly, he found himself a center of interest *(the search for the perfumed woman)* allowing him to resist this inevitable stress resulting from the loss of his bearings.

What happened to these points of reference during his absence?

Will they be where he would have left them?

Will he be able to reintegrate them into his mental scheme when he returns?

The fragrant book
© *Nathanaël AMAH , 2021 NATHAM Collection*

21

Sunday, day of the return to Paris.

Roland doesn't know where he stands anymore. His obsession for Paris no longer has the same intensity. His mission is not over.

He persists and signs.

So, a last attempt at the end of the morning is necessary, before the arrival of mom Christine.

Thus, before leaving this place, he will have put all the chances on his side, to make a success of the end of this adventure.

In the wooded area, he settled on the bench, which now became his. He knows in the slightest detail all the roughness of the wood with which it was made.

As usual, he waited, in vain.

Midday approaches.

He must return for his last meal at the guest table.

Then, without knowing why, he gets up and puts the book on the bench, exactly where he had found it.

One last look, then he turns his heels and walks away without turning around.

No sooner has he taken a few steps towards the guesthouse than he hears a woman's voice calling out to him:

The fragrant book

- « *Hey Sir, Sir!* »

He turns around and sees a young woman brandishing the book left on the bench.

- « *Sir, you forgot your book.* »

said the young woman with a broad smile but a little breathless from running towards him.

- « *Miss, this book does not belong to me. You can keep it. Good day to you and good reading!* »

Then he turns around and continues on his way to the guesthouse.

He smiles.

He has just handed over the relay.

The fragrant book

EPILOGUE

The best definition of the adventure that Roland has just experienced may be that of fatality.

Fatality:

- Character of what is fatal, of what is inevitable.

- A kind of necessity, a determination that escapes the will.

- A force that would push towards a senseless act.

To the question:

"What is fatalism? »

The answer could be :

The fragrant book

" Doctrine according to which the course of events escapes human intelligence and will, so that the destiny of each one of us would be fixed in advance by a unique and supernatural power. "

Roland, by agreeing to spend his convalescence far from Paris, was able to see that it is not so tragic to leave his comfort zone, and that it cannot be equated to a departure into exile, an uprooting, an expatriation, an extirpation.

Consequently, if one reasons irrationally, it would be quite possible to conclude that life has taken on the task of demonstrating to him the opposite of the convictions bequeathed to him by his mother.

Rationally, the advice would be that it is time to change his vision of life, that nothing is more important than to make one's own experience in order to get one's own idea on a given subject.

To all the Roland's.

End.

The fragrant book

The fragrant book

Éditeur : BoD-Books on Demand, 12/14 rond point des
Champs   Élysées,   75008   Paris,   France
Impression: BoD-Books on Demand, Norderstedt,
Allemagne
ISBN   :   **9782322229833**
Legal Deposit : February, 2021

The fragrant book